THE WOLF

G. P. Putnam's Sons / New York

WHO CRIED BOY

Story by **Bob Hartman** ∙ Pictures by **Tim Raglin**

Library of Congress Cataloging-in-Publication Data
Hartman, Bob, 1955-   The wolf who cried boy / by Bob Hartman ; illustrated by Tim Raglin.
p.   cm.   Summary: Little Wolf is tired of eating lamburgers and sloppy does, but when he tricks
his parents into thinking there is a boy in the woods, they could all miss a chance for a real feast.
[1. Wolves–Fiction. 2. Diet–Fiction.]   I. Raglin, Tim, ill. II. Title.   PZ7.H26725 Wo 2002
E–dc21 2001019604   ISBN 0-399-23578-7
10 9 8 7 6 5 4 3 2

to Eli – B. H.

for Mary Alice and Chuck! – T. R.

Once upon a time

there lived a family of wolves. They stole sheep, ran after deer, and snacked on muskrat and squirrel.

Except for Little Wolf, that is, who never stopped complaining about what his mother prepared each night for dinner.

"Lamburgers again?" he whined. "I hate Lamburgers!"

"Sloppy Does?" he howled. "We had Sloppy Does last night!"

"Chocolate Moose?" he whimpered. "Chocolate Moose makes me sick.
And besides, it looks just like—"

"That's enough!"
barked Father Wolf.
But it never did any good, for all
Little Wolf wanted to eat was . . .

"**Boy!** Why can't we have Boy tonight? We never have Boy anymore!"

"Well, son," sighed Father Wolf, "there was a time when a clever wolf could snatch a shepherd boy off a hill or pluck a farm boy out of a field. Why, there was nothing better than a steaming plate of **Boy Chops,**  a big **Baked Boy-tato,** and some **Boys-n-Berry Pie.** But boys are hard to come by these days, so stop your complaining and finish off that Moose."

"Yes, Father," Little Wolf muttered. Then he asked, "But suppose I did find a boy someday?"

Father Wolf smiled. "You find a boy out there in the woods, and your mother and I will be happy to catch him and cook him for you. But I wouldn't get my hopes up if I were you."

The next day, as Little Wolf made his way home from school, he sniffed the air.

"Three-Pig Salad!" he moaned. "I hate Three-Pig Salad!" And then Little Wolf remembered what his father had told him about catching a boy someday. So he decided to play a little trick, and put off that awful dinner for a while. He ran home just as fast as he could, howling all the way.

"Boy! Boy! I've just seen a boy in the woods! If we hurry, we can catch him!"

Father and
Mother Wolf
raced
out of the cave.
They **ran**
through the woods
to the top of the hill
and all the way down to the creek.
They **peered**
into trees
and **sniffed**
behind rocks
and **looked**
into every hollow log.

But they could not find the boy.

"We looked **everywhere**," panted Father Wolf. "Everywhere a boy might go. But we just couldn't find him. Better luck next time, Son."

Little Wolf tried to look disappointed, but it was all he could do to keep from laughing.

The joke got even better when his mother announced,
"Oh no! The Three-Pig Salad is ruined! The bricks are limp,
the straw is damp, and the sticks have turned all . . . sticky."

"Don't worry, dear," Father Wolf said. "We can make do
with snack food tonight."

And so they

crunched on

Chipmunks and Dip,

and Little Wolf was happy.

So happy, in fact, that he decided to try the same trick the very next day.

"It's the boy!" he cried. "I saw him again! He's just at the edge of the woods!"

So, once again, Father and Mother Wolf went racing after the boy. Once again, they came dragging home, their paws empty. And, once again, their dinner was ruined.

"Just look at that Granny Smith Pie," Mother Wolf sighed. "The apples are entirely too mushy."

"Yep," agreed Father Wolf. "And Granny's gone all crusty and hard."

"Looks like snacks again tonight." Little Wolf shrugged.

But the **smile** on his face made Father Wolf wonder—
and then he heard his son, a little later, on the phone.

"That's right," Little Wolf whispered, "I didn't have to eat
dinner tonight either! I think I'll tell them there's a boy out
there tomorrow, too!"

Father Wolf went straight to Mother Wolf, and they agreed
that on the following night, they would **ignore**
his silly tricks.

The next day, Little Wolf made his way home from school as usual. He could smell the awful odor of hot steaming Muskratatouille as it floated out of the cave, and was just about to holler "Boy!" when the most amazing thing happened.

There, walking through the woods before him, were

more boys than he had ever seen!

"**Boy!**" he cried. "Boy!" But no one came running from the cave.

"Boy!" he howled. "**BOYS!**" But still no one came.
So he ran into the cave, shouting, "There are boys out there!
Dozens of them!
Big ones and little ones.
Fat ones and skinny ones.
Enough to fill our freezer and Auntie's
freezer, too!"
But his mother just shrugged and said,
"That's very nice, dear, but I already
have our supper planned."
Father Wolf hid his face
behind a newspaper.

And that's when one of the boys stuck his head in the cave.

He was the mischievous type—a lot like Little Wolf, in fact. And he had crept away from his Scout pack to have a closer look.

"**See!**" Little Wolf shouted.

"There's one of them now!"

But even though the boy tiptoed right into the cave, Little Wolf couldn't get anyone to look.

"**There's a boy on the couch!**" he howled.

"That's enough now, Son," said his mother.

"You're not fooling us again," added his father from behind the paper. "We're on to your little tricks."

"But I'm not lying this time. Honest!" Little Wolf pleaded.

"There really is a boy—right here, in our cave!" The boy glanced at his watch, then turned to leave.

"Look! Please look!" Little Wolf begged. "He's getting away!" But by the time Father Wolf finally stuck his head up above the paper, the boy was gone.

"You waited too long!" cried Little Wolf. "He was here a minute ago. All we have to do is run outside—"

"We will do no such thing!" growled Father Wolf. "From now on, you will eat your dinner without complaining."

"And you will stop your fibbing, once and for all!" said his mother. "Do you understand?"

"Okay," Little Wolf sighed.

So from then on, Little Wolf ate Lamburgers and Three-Pig Salad and even grew fond of Granny Smith Pie. And he never, ever cried "Boy!" again!

And that's why the boys, at least, lived happily ever after!